THE BRAVE COWBOY

JOAN WALSH ANGLUND

HARCOURT BRACE JOVANOVICH

NEW YORK AND LONDON

A VOYAGER BOOK

For my own little cowboy, Todd

Printed in the United States of America

Library of Congress Cataloging in Publication Data
Anglund, Joan Walsh.
  The brave cowboy.
  (A Voyager book ; AVB 104)
  SUMMARY: *Imaginary adventures with Indians,*
wild animals, and outlaws keep a little cowboy
busy.
  [1. Cowboys—Fiction] I. Title.
PZ7.A586Br7   [E]   76-15638
ISBN *0-15-614050-0*

First Voyager edition 1976
A B C D E F G H I J

THE BRAVE COWBOY

Once there was a cowboy.

He was strong and brave.
He was not afraid of coyotes.
He was not afraid of Indians.
He was not afraid of ornery rustlers.

He stood tall and straight...and had a two-holster belt.

Each morning he would eat breakfast . . .

brush his teeth . . .

and feed the cat.

Each day he put on his hat . . .

pulled on his boots . . .

and buckled on his two-holster belt.

Sometimes, he would set out to find
a camp of rustlers to round them up
and put them in jail. . . .

Or, maybe he would hunt wild Indians that might be in the territory. . . .

Or, maybe he would shoot a rattlesnake . . .

or capture an angry mountain lion . . .

or just take a ride across the prairie.

He was always busy.
He had much to do.
He must bring in provisions . . .

rescue fair maidens in distress . . .

warn the stagecoach that the bridge was out.

Sometimes things went well for the cowboy . . .
when he was made deputy sheriff
by the people of the town . . .

when he led the covered wagons
across the plains . . .

when he won first prize
at the rodeo.

And sometimes he had troubles . . .
when his tent collapsed while he was camping out . . .

when he ran out of food on the trail,
far away from camp . . .

when his horse went lame while he was hunting buffalo. . . .

But he was never baffled . . .
he was not afraid . . .
and he never gave up.

And so, when night fell on the prairie
and the coyotes howled at the moon,
the tired cowboy . . .

took off his boots . . .

hung up his hat . . .

and unbuckled his two-holster belt.

He said his prayers . . .
climbed in his bunk . . .

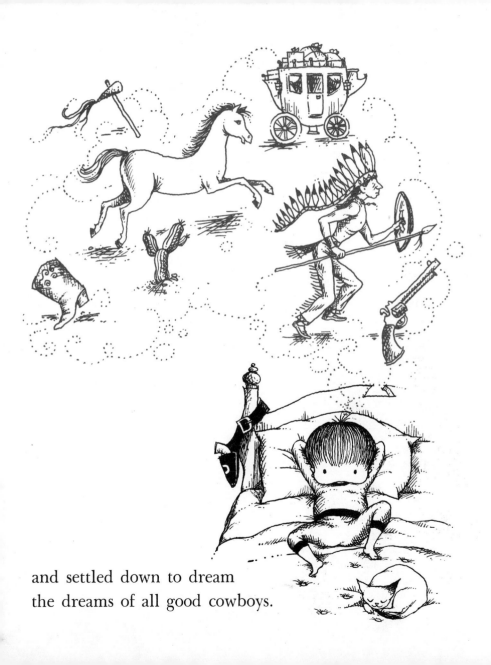

and settled down to dream
the dreams of all good cowboys.

Good night little cowboy. . . . Sweet dreams.